IN SHADOW I BLOOM

SHIRLEY SIATON PARABIA

In Shadow I Bloom
Poetry and Short Fiction

Copyright © 2024 Shirley Siaton Parabia

ALL RIGHTS RESERVED.

No part of this book may be reproduced or used in any manner without the prior written permission of the copyright owner, except for the use of brief quotations in a book review. To request permission, contact the publisher at books@inkysword.com.

This is a work of fiction. Names, characters, businesses, events and incidents are the products of the author's imagination. Any resemblance to actual persons, living or dead, or actual events is purely coincidental.

All brand and product names used in this book are trademarks, registered trademarks, or trade names of their respective owners. Inky Sword Book Publishing is not associated with any product or vendor in this book.

ISBN 978-621-8371-60-6 (paperback)

First Edition, December 2024

Published by Shirley S. Parabia
Cover by Janina Cover Designs
Interior formatting by Champagne Book Design
Illustrations by Rein Geronimo

Inky Sword Book Publishing
Barangay Quezon, Arevalo, Iloilo City 5000
Republic of the Philippines
inkysword.com

CONTENT WARNINGS

Warning for mentions of violence and substance use.

Recommended for readers 12 years old and above.

You

Yes, ***you***

Never be afraid to be you

There's no one else who could be

You

CONTENTS

Content Warnings iii
Acknowledgments ix
The Collection xi

Life 1
Won't 3

A Fire in the Soul 5
Foreword 11
Chapter One 13
Chapter Two 17
Chapter Three 21
Chapter Four 25
Chapter Five 29
Chapter Six 31
Words To Know 33

Screen 37
Home 39

Hobo 41
Foreword 47
Chapter One 49
Chapter Two 57

Shoes 61
Stone 65

About the Author 69
On the Web 71

ACKNOWLEDGMENTS

I am very grateful to *Glitter Magazine Philippines, Estudyante Network Magazine,* and *The Philippine Star* for taking a chance on an unknown kid and giving her short fiction and poetry the opportunity to be read the world over.

THE COLLECTION

This book sprang forth from an idea that my mother came up with during one of our online chats in early 2023. More specifically, she thought it would be the bee's knees if I shared my literary pieces to a wider audience.

Well, here you go, Ma.

This particular collection was curated for a young adult audience, showcasing poems and stories written while I was around the same age. It was fun being able to look back at the perspective and voice I had during these youthful years.

One thing I learned and valued the most from my entire writing journey was that I stayed true to the *me* behind the words that you now see in print.

It was the *me* who saw life as something beautiful on the whole—sometimes dark, sometimes bright, oftentimes challenging, but always filled with rays of hope and determination that helped me grow as, well, *me*.

POETRY AND SHORT FICTION

life

You matter.

Your art is beautiful.
Your story transcends worlds.
Your voice deserves to be heard.

Your hands shape the future.
Your love will make someone believe in themselves—
that includes you.

Your heart beats life.

won't

I will not apologize

For my power
My strength and my drive

For my appetite
My ambition and my desires

For my love
My emotions and my regrets

I will not apologize
For all that make me
Me

A FIRE IN THE SOUL

I am not a warrior.

My name is Uryana. I am twelve cycles old and a child of the *Baraw* tribe from the *Sa-Babaw* peaks.

My people have been plagued by the Serpent, a beast made of flame. It first devoured our livestock, then burned our fields and orchards to ashes.

Our strongest warriors were called to face this creature, but each of them, including my own father, met their end at its merciless jaws.

I was chosen by our tribe Elders to fight the Serpent. Will I be seeing my final dusk tonight, or will the hope and fire in my heart be enough to guide me in my greatest battle?

FOREWORD

I wrote the first version of this story literally at the turn of the century, in January 2000.

Uryana and the Baraw tribe had long since dwelt in my imagination in a sort of neo-reality between ancient and modern Philippine mythology.

In 2023, I thought of writing a children's book for my daughters Arya, a voracious reader, and Selene, born on the 30th of April that year.

Who best to write about than young Uryana, the fleet-footed Anak-ni-Pandukaw, who fearlessly faced the greatest foe of her people? She wasn't a trained warrior, but, boy, did she bring the fight!

Fire of Courage came to life then, illustrated by Rozy Clemente and Rein Geronimo, and was released in May 2023.

CHAPTER ONE

SA-BABAW

"You are the Chosen One."

To this very day, these words echo through my mind whenever I look at the mountains of home.

I live in *Sa-Babaw,* a vast mountain range with the highest of peaks, the most mysterious of forests, the most dangerous of paths.

Sa-Babaw is a place of convergence.

This is where the most powerful magical forces of the land breed, where *kapre* dwell in the tallest trees of our gardens, where creatures from the underworld such as *diwata* and *duwende* sometimes visit to trade, and where the sunrise is first seen.

Today that beauty is no more.

Our entire tribe, the fierce and agile *Baraw,* has been plagued by a half-seen, evil creature called the Serpent.

It first devoured our entire livestock, then burned our fields and orchards to ashes.

The strongest of men were gathered to face this creature, but each of them met their end at its merciless jaws.

My name is Uryana. I am the only child of one of *Sa-Babaw*'s most powerful warriors, Pandukaw. He, too, met his last breath in mortal combat against the Serpent.

When the number of able-bodied *Baraw* men slowly dwindled to a handful, the Elders gathered round the village's *Tutod*, the enchanted bonfire that never went out even in the most violent of storms, and prayed fervently for salvation to the *anito*.

Then the *Apo*, the oldest and wisest man in our village, shouted for everyone to hear that *Anak-ni-Pandukaw* was the one destined to face the Serpent, as the *Tutod* said to them.

That was me.

CHAPTER TWO

CHOSEN

"Y͟OU ARE THE C͟HOSEN O͟NE, U͟RYANA A͟NAK-NI-P͟ANDUKAW. What say you?"

I stared at the wrinkled, brittle face of the *Apo*.

Was this meant to be some kind of trick or joke?

Perhaps the Elders have gone mad. How could they even believe that I, a girl of no more than twelve cycles, was the one destined to fight the Serpent?

"*Apo*, I am not a warrior." I stood before the Elders, who all looked back at me with blank, unblinking eyes.

The *Apo* pursed his rubbery lips. "Ah. But are you not the fastest runner of the *Baraw* people?"

"The gods have gifted me with light feet, *Apo*, not hands that could easily draw blood."

The *Apo* roared with laughter. "The Serpent has no blood, foolish child! It is a creature of fire, not of flesh and soul!"

"Is that why the warriors–even my father–could not defeat it?"

"Yes. Their spears, arrows and knives all melted."

I could almost hear the screams of the warriors as their souls fought to remain in their mortal flesh. "I see."

For a moment, I looked around at the children, women, and elderly men left in the village.

I had no idea how to become their savior.

"Then…then…I accept, *Apo*."

Chapter Three

TRABUNGKO

I stood on *Bato-talum*, a sharp and jagged piece of rock jutting from the depths of the earth and overlooking *Baraw* lands.

I looked at the horizon as it took the last rays of the sun into its embrace. I prayed fervently to the *anito* that this would not be my final dusk.

"Uryana?"

I looked at my mother, Sulaya. She was removing a leather rawhide string from around her neck. I saw that it was a necklace–my father's necklace. From the string hung a shiny, light-colored, round jewel.

"That is my father's, is it not?"

"Yes." My mother fastened the string around my neck.

"It is a talisman. A *trabungko*. Its light is from the essence of the Serpent. It has fire within, fire that would give you the Serpent's own strength, fire that would make you defeat the Serpent. Your father…he gave it to me before he left to fight his final battle."

I felt the sharp coldness of the jewel of fire as I touched it. I also felt the icy steel of the spear I carried across my back.

Everything felt cold, as I thought of what I was about to face.

"Mother, it is best you leave now. It is nightfall. Soon, the Serpent will come here to *Bato-talum*, to look over the land and see where it could next strike."

"May the *anito* watch over you, *anak*."

"Thank you, Mother." I watched her leave, scurrying to the safety of the village.

If her eyes shed the tears, my own heart cried in return.

CHAPTER FOUR

SERPENT

Once the final ray of sunlight melted into the shadows, the Serpent appeared right beside my rocky perch.

It was made not of scales, as snakes should be, but of fire, a molten swirl of claws and tentacles and fangs.

"Ssss. *Anak-ni-Pandukaw.*"

I backed away from it, feeling its scorching breath against my skin. The sight of the ghastly creature almost melted my resolve to fight.

It laughed; a high, echoing cackle that seemed to come from the depths of the underworld.

"Sssss. You are afraid of my fire? Hasss…hassss…hasssss…"

The fire from the Serpent's molten body made something on my chest flash. I looked down and saw the *trabungko*, gleaming with its own power.

Fire that would make me defeat the serpent.

I felt its power surge through my veins, filling my soul with white-hot strength and hope.

I planted my feet firmly on the ground. "I, too, have that same kind of fire."

And I, Uryana the Swift, ran through the forest.

The jewel on my necklace lit the path. Heedless to the Serpent chasing me, heedless that it was one breath away from burning me to the next life, I followed the *trabungko*'s guiding light.

I reached a cliff. It gaped towards the open sea, the blue-black-white canvas of tossing sounds and salty foam. Far below, the water crashed against the sharp rocks of the coast.

There was no other path but the one through which I ran.

I saw the Serpent slithering down the path towards me, hissing as it did, burning everything in its wake.

It is a being of fire, not of flesh and soul.

I grabbed the *trabungko* from my neck and held it against the night sky. The jewel shone like a tiny full moon in my hand.

"Here, Serpent. Take your strength with you."

The Serpent pounced at my bait. It leapt through the air, trailing balls of fire, as it greedily dove for the *trabungko*.

I swiftly ducked out of its path, sending the molten

A FIRE IN THE SOUL

creature down the cliff, straight into the cold, salty foam of the sea.

The water hungrily devoured the fire, putting it out, allowing darkness to fall over the cliffs like a blanket.

I knew, then, that it was over.

CHAPTER FIVE

STRENGTH

"You are indeed the Chosen One, Uryana." My mother met me with a hug after the Elders had sung me songs of praise before the *Tutod*.

"No, mother. The *trabungko* did it. It was Father's talisman that made me win. It gave me the strength to defeat the Serpent."

My mother laughed as she had never laughed before.

"You are indeed a foolish child, Uryana! That was a piece of shiny rock from the stream, not a trabungko! It was your father's, yes, but it had no special powers."

I was dumbstruck. "Why did you tell me–?"

"Just before you were born, an *ermintanya* told me that I would have a warrior-child with great fire in its heart and soul."

"You were only trying to–"

My mother nodded. "It took something to let the fire in you come out. But it was there inside of you all along."

CHAPTER SIX

HEART

Now I stand on Bato-talum, bearing witness to yet another dusk.

I fiddle with the shiny rock in my hand and watch its surface gleam brightly against the waning rays of the sun.

I take off the necklace and put it in my pocket. Then I listen to the beating of my heart.

It is here where the fire has always been.

WORDS TO KNOW

Anak
Child; son or daughter
'Anak ni Pandukaw' means 'Child of Pandukaw'

Anito
Ancestor spirits, nature spirits and deities

Apo
Patriarch; chief elder man of a tribe

Bato-Talum
Bato means 'rock,' 'talum' means 'sharp'

Diwata
A spirit or lesser god/goddess who guards natural features such as forests

Duwende
A dwarf or goblin

Ermitanya
A female hermit, usually with the powers of a shaman/oracle

Kapre

A tree giant, described to be very tall, dark and hairy

Sa-Babaw

Babaw means 'top,' from a place of height
Literally translates to 'On top'

Trabungko

A snake stone; usually spherical in shape and glows in the dark, said to have healing powers

Tutod

Burning; the act of burning, commonly a bonfire

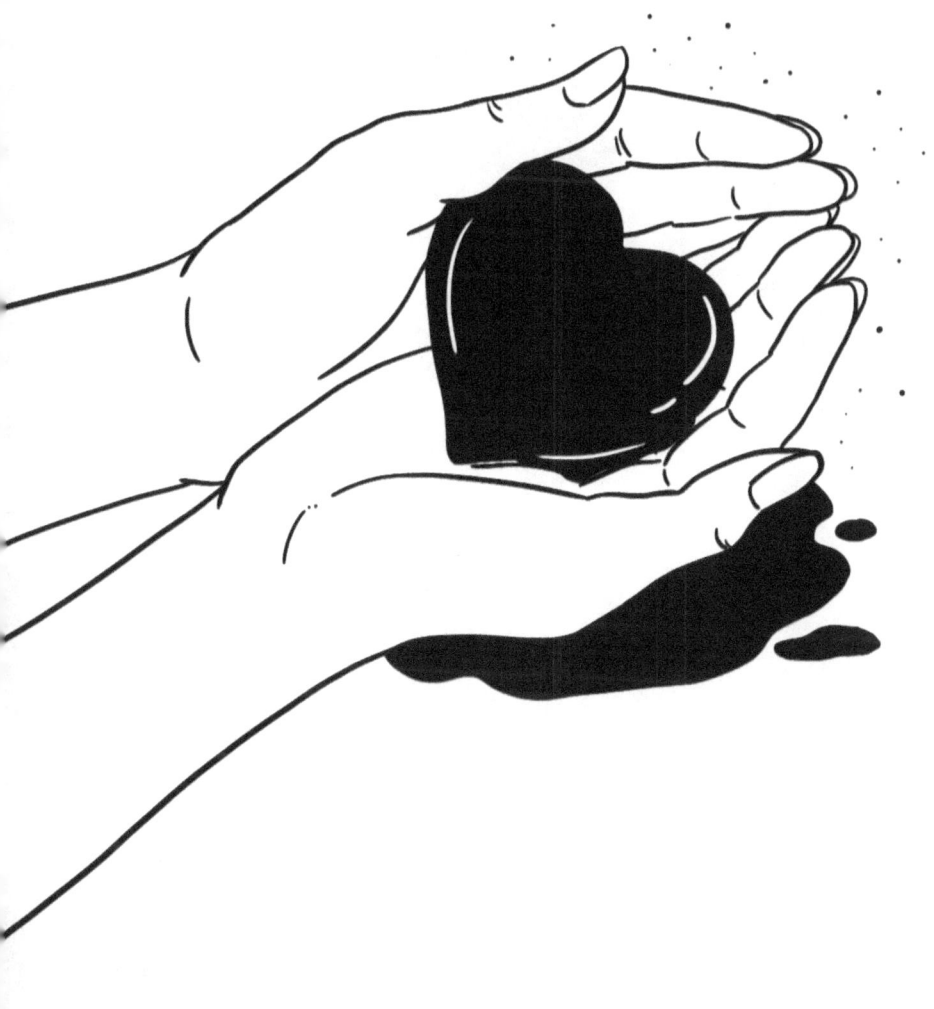

screen

I still look at the screen
Hoping it would be your message
Hoping somehow you found me

I still look at the screen
Hoping your picture would be there
Happy, smiling, truly alive

With tears in my eyes
In the quiet hours of dawn
Though I know
You will never be there

I still look at the screen

home

I want to go home

To the days of years past
When the breeze was soft
Laughter was easy
Love was a possibility

To the days that never were
When I saw you
Found you
Loved you

To the days when you were there
When I had your voice
Your light
Your heartbeat

I want to go home

HOBO

How could I forget him?

He became my special friend at the intersection that night.
He was endearing and magical.

I'd like to think we felt the same.
We didn't want to let each other go.

FOREWORD

This is the first mature short story I had written in my mid-teens and eventually had published, a simple interaction between two disparate souls in a gritty street corner.

The dialogue herein consists of colloquial Filipino language, with the English translation provided right after in italics.

It had since taken the form of a darkly poignant love story, the novella *Angel* (August 2023).

CHAPTER ONE

SKY

I gazed at the sky for probably the umpteenth time in the past hour.

It was a starry night. The North Star and the many known constellations could easily be made out against the clear blue-black canvas of the heavens. The moon was full and perfectly spherical, possessing the magic of the New Year and a roaring fire.

My gaze reverted back to the sidewalk where I was sitting by myself on a freshly painted bench by the bus stop. It was in the corner of my favorite intersection. The green, red, yellow, orange and blue lights given off by the store neons and the traffic light hung overhead cast a cheery, eerie glow on the stone pavement. The street was littered with newspapers and flyers, and tarnished by graffiti.

I gazed at the sky again. This time, it seemed to have grown murky, cloudy, as if the lights cast by the celestial bodies were suddenly spirited away.

As my hopes had been.

I went to this bench by the intersection almost two hours ago: expectant, eager, because the boy of my dreams had called me up earlier in the afternoon and asked if I could go to the movies with him. I said yes almost instantly. Moving on Cloud 9, I put on my best dress and new shoes and snuck into my mom's room to borrow her makeup and use a little spritz of expensive perfume.

Obvious as it was, one could already tell what occurred. But I'll say it straight: he stood me up.

That scumbag Fidel stood me up.

It was getting cold. My watch said it was already half past eight in the evening. I pulled my now-rumpled white cardigan closer around my shoulders, tugging at the edges like I would if I got a cord somehow tied around *his* neck. I swear that smoke was already coming out of my nostrils.

Puff. Puff. Puff.

Damn it.

"Inindyan ka? Dalawang oras na."

Stood you up, hasn't he? It's been two hours.

I jumped up, ready to defend myself against that person who so rascally intruded on my thoughts and scared the socks off of me.

The voice came from behind the street bench. I

turned a hundred and eighty degrees, already poised on my feet.

The rainbow glow of the evening lights illuminated a slightly shrouded silhouette beneath the awning of an ice cream shop.

It was a young man. He clearly looked like he belonged on the streets. His clothes and his knit cap were tattered.

"Sino ka?"

Who are you?

My question sounded like a shriek, a sound that mirrored both my fright and irritation. That person had some nerve to startle me!

He emerged from the shadows, grinning, showing even pearly whites. I could see he was no older than my eighteen years, or perhaps he was in his early twenties. He had eyes as dark as the sky and hair as thick as a wild animal's mane, wavy locks peeking out from beneath the cap.

The street light showed deep-brown skin, and a body used to hard work. The tattered outfit did not clash with his appeal, instead, it enhanced his appearance in a, well…*stylish* sort of way.

Immediately, I softened up. Nobody could stay mad too long at someone so…so…*cute.*

Okay. He was cute.

He grinned at me broadly.

"Ako si Trey."

I am Trey.

I merely nodded. Regaining my composure, I plopped on the bench, trying my best to ignore him as calmly as I could.

But Trey slid into the seat beside me, taking off his cap. Up close, I made out that he probably had some foreign blood that gave him sharp, exotic looks. He had eyes that swept up at the corners, and lean, hard features.

For someone off the streets, he looked better, a hell of a lot better, than Fidel.

He looked at me curiously.

"Ano'ng pangalan mo?"

What's your name?

"Stella," I replied, trying to concentrate on the cars passing us by on the road.

He held out a cup. It looked to be steaming hot, and filled with what could only be coffee.

"Gusto mo ng kape?"

Would you like some coffee?

A stranger's openness would usually irritate me, but strangely, I wasn't offended by him. He seemed sincere and trustworthy. Besides, it wasn't like he was trying to pick me up or something. Besides, a girl my age could very well take care of herself.

I smiled at such an unusual gesture. Something inside me said I could trust this guy. "Mukhang masarap. Pero, salamat na lang."

It looks delicious. But, no, thanks.

He nodded and proceeded to sip his coffee.

Silence.

I couldn't help but notice his thin, tattered clothing and how his body would react to the crisp January air. "Masyadong malamig. Hindi ka ba giniginaw niyan?"

It's freezing. Aren't you cold?

He shook his head, seemingly lost in his own thoughts.

A moment later, his expression changed. He was smiling at me.

"Hindi darating si Fidel ano?"

Fidel isn't coming, is he?

I frowned and gritted my teeth. I asked him how he knew the name of my would-be date.

He shrugged and spoke matter-of-factly. "Kilala ko siya. Barkada siya ng isang kasamahan ko. Bumibili yan ng MJ."

I know him. He's friends with one of the guys from here. He buys marijuana.

Our school's star basketball player—a marijuana user?

I suddenly wanted to lash out at him in defense of

my future boyfriend…but, to be honest, Fidel was from the popular crowd, among those who had always taken me for granted on campus. It was a wonder why he'd even asked me out in the first place.

Then I recalled one of my classmates telling me that there was a nasty rumor going around that Fidel was a drug user.

In a whispery voice, Trey explained to me that several girls had waited for Fidel in the exact same spot by the intersection, but he never came.

I was bewildered. "Totoo?"

For real?

"Oo. Parang trip yatang paghintayin ng taong 'yon ang mga tsiks dito at ibangko. Tapos, alam mo, may isang babae nga rito, hindi nadala nu'ng unang beses, nakipagkita pa rin siya. Ayun, inindiyan uli. Ayaw niyang maniwala sa 'kin na hindi darating si Fidel. Minura pa nga niya ako, at ipapupulis daw. Gusto ko lang naman makatulong, e."

Yes. He seems to have a thing for having girls come here, and then standing them up. And, you know, there's this one girl, she didn't learn the first time, and she came right back. He stood her up again. She shouted at me and threatened to have the cops arrest me. I just wanted to help.

The light in his midnight eyes was warm, friendly, and strangely comforting. We talked for a few more minutes—about my school, about how he came to live on the streets.

I learned that he left home years ago because he couldn't stand his stepfather beating him up. He stayed at his friend's place. Did all kinds of jobs. One thing he said he'd never attempted was peddling – or doing – drugs.

It was getting late and we both knew it.

He smiled at me, a bit ruefully. "Baka...hinahanap ka na sa inyo."

Maybe...they're already worried about you at home.

I hesitated before nodding.

He offered to walk me home. As people stared to look at this typical schoolgirl cheerfully strolling with a street kid by her side, I simply did not care.

That night, I felt that we were more than just new friends. As we walked away from the intersection, we were a handsomely-dressed couple headed for the Ball of the Century.

CHAPTER TWO

NOBODY

It was two days later when I stopped by at the bench after my classes, to perhaps see him, or maybe just say hello.

He wasn't there.

I asked around. I spoke with the street vendors and those who lurked in the shadows of the nearby alleys.

Nobody knew who Trey was.

I came back a few more times, mostly in the evenings, hoping against hope he would somehow turn up.

He never did.

I never saw him again.

shoes

The soles antediluvian
of my hollow being sustain
with silent patience, or patient silence
the blunt end
of your insecurities and neuroses

Have you ever thought
of the beatings I get
from cruel concrete pavements
and wooden floors that reek
of lemon-scented dye wax?

The stat book of all the
fouls I received against debris and rocks
had long since been deluged
by both defensive and offensive kinds
even the technicals
Sadly, I drew no shots, just bruises from impact
that left me more empty than ever
And pained

I endure the stench
of your human inadequacies
take time out to absorb
the wetness that streaks from your flesh
like tears

Sweat

There are the clumps of gum
their sugary sweetness chewed out
dog waste, and even the toffee candy
from a faraway land
that you didn't like

You were too enraptured with the sights ahead
to look down once in a while
at the path you tread.

Times came that you outgrew me
or gave me away to less-classy *promdi* relatives
or I was just too worn
to show off anymore

Your tootsies' humble sheath
I am at your bidding
My life is subject to your whims

Once I was a pair of boots with spurs
then suede pumps, and docksiders
Now–for now–I'm your overpriced basketball shoes
With someone's name

Not yours

stone

Stolen from the aria
Of crashing forest waters,
Ripped like a body's heart;
A-bleeding
A stone.

Stories of war shattered
Long since;
Dead hearts wielding
World War II's disease
Inside.

From a trouser pocket
(roaches' mealy meat)
With a basketball cut-out sked
The stone was taken
From past distant.

Journeyed leagues
Countless hours and interminable sunsets.
A grandson
Who watched Power Rangers;
His legacy.

Put in carelessly
A faux Bulls shorts pocket,
Jordan, twenty-three,
And bet jolen dozens
Lost all
The once-mossy rock along.

Left the asphalt byway
To watch yet another game on TV.
Left a legacy
Trampled, rolling:
It bounced away.

The stone.

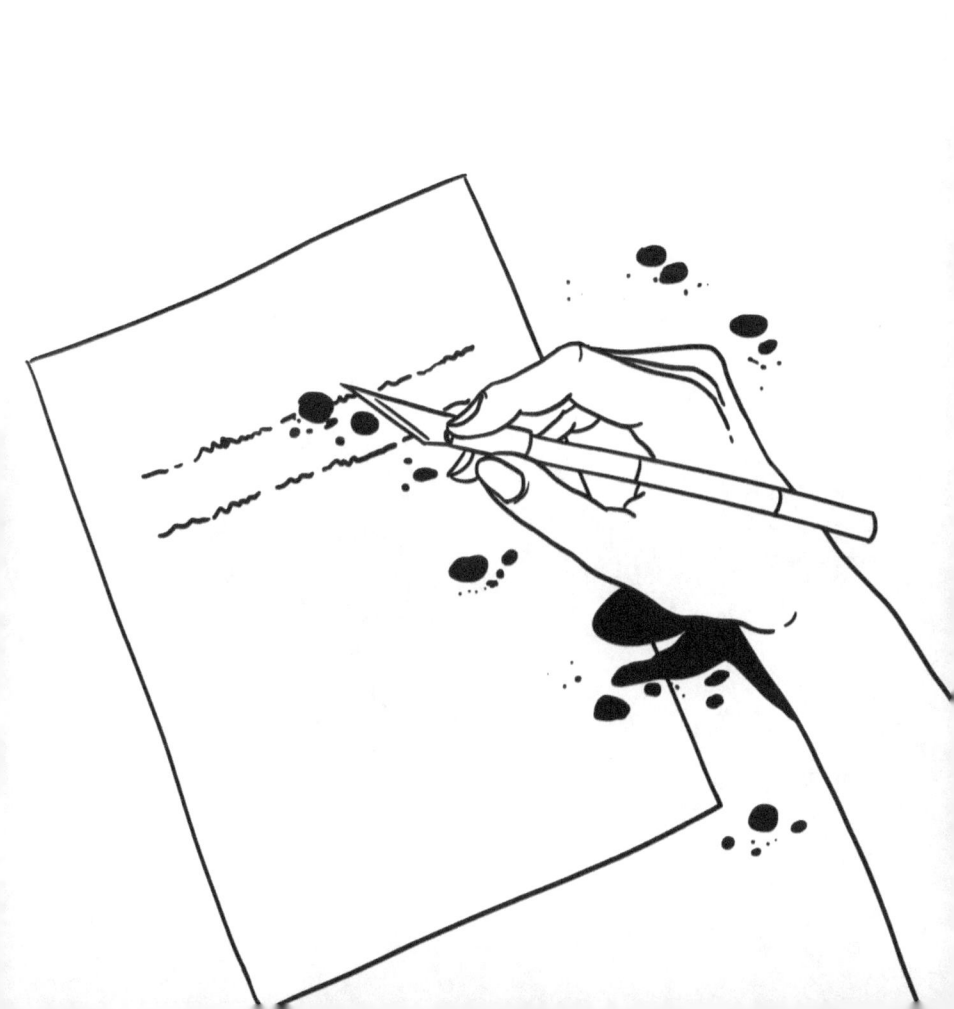

ABOUT THE AUTHOR

Shirley Siaton Parabia writes edgy and evocative novels and poems. Her worlds are in a deliciously dark cross-section of the romance, neo-noir, action, fantasy, new adult, and contemporary genres.

She has several books of fiction and poetry released since February 2023. Her first book is the free verse collection *Black Cat and other poems*.

She is an award-winning writer, poet, and journalist in English, Filipino, and Hiligaynon, lauded by the Stevan Javellana Foundation, Philippine Information Agency, and West Visayas State University. Her essays, short stories, and poems have been published internationally in print and digital media. Her multi-lingual plays have been staged in the Philippines.

Shirley is a black belt in Shotokan Karate and an international certified fitness coach. She has a Master's degree in Public Administration and a career in international education. Originally from Iloilo City, she lives in the Middle East with her husband and two daughters.

ON THE WEB

Shirley's official website:
shirleysiaton.com

Complete reading guide:
shirley.pub

Subscribe to Shirley's VIP list for free exclusive updates:
newsletter.shirleysiaton.com

www.ingramcontent.com/pod-product-compliance
Lightning Source LLC
LaVergne TN
LVHW090036080526
838202LV00046B/3840